SUDEEP BANERJEE

THE GREAT TALES OF TERRIBLE ASURAS

Cuckoo TALES

An Imprint of
Srishti Publishers & Distributors

Srishti Publishers & Distributors

A unit of AJR Publishing LLP
212A, Peacock Lane
Shahpur Jat, New Delhi – 110 049
editorial@srishtipublishers.com

First published by
Srishti Publishers & Distributors in 2022

10 9 8 7 6 5 4 3 2 1

The stories have been researched and retold for children, with no intent of hurting anyone's sentiments. The author asserts the moral right to be identified as the author of this work.

Printed and bound in India.

Salutations to Ma Kali who empowers my will.

This book is lovingly dedicated to:

My grandmother, Kalyani Bhattacharya,

My parents, Sondhya Banerjee and Bimal Banerjee,

My dear Sudipta di and Kalyan da,

And to Pukun (Adidev).

I'm grateful for your love and blessings.

Author's note

Hold on! Before you dive into the book, let me steal a few minutes from you. Don't worry, it will not take hours! The book you are holding right now comprises a collection of stories which are completely centred upon the anti-heroes of Hindu mythology, whom we tend to call *asuras.* Tell me something, have you ever wondered why do we call them asuras? Or, how they were born? Or what was their relationship with gods or devas? Allow me to explain the matter.

According to Hindu mythology, the world is governed by Tridev or the trio of three gods – Brahma, Vishnu and Shiva. Brahma is the Creator. He builds everything you see around the world and across the universe. He is called the "Father of Creation". Vishnu is the Preserver. He protects everything that Brahma has created, hence, he is called the "Preserver of the Universe". And Shiva is the Destroyer. He destroys everything that has been created and preserved by Brahma and Vishnu, as destruction is needed for a new beginning. He is called the "Destroyer of Evil" and the "God of all gods – Mahadeva".

Although there are many other great gods, Brahma, Vishnu and Shiva are the main gods among them. Together, they are the symbol of oneness, which is called the Trinity or Trio. In the primary stage of creation, when Brahma created every living and non-living being, he also created a mighty sage named Kashyap, who had two wives – Diti and Aditi.

When both the women bore the sage's children, the sons of Aditi were called Adityas, who were later renowned as devas; while Diti's sons were called asuras. The devas and asuras were stepbrothers, and by the grace of lord Brahma, they thrived and became powerful superhumans. But as time skittered, the devas became more benevolent and peace-bringing, while the asuras became power-seekers. And this dual quality ensued rage and enmity between the two. They started competing against each other. And from then on, the asuras devoted their existence to ruin the lives of devas. They used to seek boons from the Trinity of gods and abused their powers to cause havoc in the lives of devas.

However, no matter how powerful they got, they could never stand against the might and intelligence of the devas. They ended up being defeated all the time. Nevertheless, their amazing stories always make us laugh, leaving us wondering how nasty the asuras could be!

Here are some great stories of the mighty asuras, who troubled the gods and humans, and became the supreme anti-heroes in most of our mythological stories. Now that you know all this, you are allowed to devour the entire book!

Contents

1

THE BROTHERS WHO TURNED INTO ASURAS

Lord Vishnu is known as the preserver of the universe, who sustains living and non-living beings around the world. He resides in Vaikuntha loka, where he can be found meditating, lying on the coils of Adi-Sesha – the giant snake with a thousand heads. Since the beginning of time, Jaya and Vijaya – two divine beings – used to guard Vaikuntha loka. They were twin brothers and were ardent devotees of Vishnu.

The brothers were very sincere and dedicated in performing their duties. They would hardly permit anyone to enter the lord's house. Vishnu also didn't want anyone to disturb him during his meditation and was happy with his guards. But one day, the four Kumara brothers appeared, all at once! The Kumara brothers were the four dwarf sages – Sanaka Kumara, Sanandana Kumara, Sanatana Kumara and Sanat Kumara. They were born out of Brahma's head and were as learned as Brahma himself. But unlike Brahma, they had the tendency to get angry if they were not treated respectfully. Everyone was aware of their nature, so they respected them. They were scared to face their fury, because when the Kumaras got angry, disasters followed.

As soon as the Kumara brothers reached the doorstep of Vishnu's abode, they saw Jaya and Vijaya. They calmly said, 'O Jaya and Vijaya, the ardent devotees of lord Vishnu! We are here to meet the lord, and would like to have a little conversation with him. Kindly let us go in.'

But Jaya and Vijaya raised their hands, stopping them at the entry gate. They said, 'O mighty sages, our lord is meditating right now, so we are not allowed to let anyone go inside. Please wait here until the lord finishes his meditation.' But that was too much for the four brothers to handle. Out of immense anger, they warned, 'Don't oppose the Kumara brothers or you'll have to pay a terrible price for such disobedience. Let us go in, and we assure you that we won't disturb the lord.' Jaya and Vijaya were well aware that opposing the sages would mean terrible consequences for them. But at the same time, they were obliged to perform their duty to Vishnu, no matter what. So they stood their ground and didn't let them go inside.

This infuriated the sages, and they shouted, 'You fools! How dare you stop us! We curse you both to leave Vaikuntha loka forever. You will be forced to live among the mortals on earth. You would never be able to meet your lord again!' The curse was so terrible that Jaya and Vijaya panicked. They started praying to lord Vishnu desperately.

Vishnu appeared at the gate soon after. Jaya and Vijaya's ardent prayers and panic had led him out. He was surprised to learn about the whole event. Turning towards Jaya and Vijaya, he said, 'My dear devotees, no one can undo the curse of the Kumara brothers. Unfortunately, I won't be able to protect you. But since you are my devotees, I can soften the curse a bit. I can give you two options against the curse – either you can choose to spend seven lifetimes on earth being my devotees, or you can choose to be my enemies for three lifetimes.'

Jaya and Vijaya didn't want to stay away from their lord for long. They both revered Vishnu the most, so they chose to become his enemies for three lifetimes. 'So be it!' Vishnu said and smiled. He blessed them with their choice.And from then on, the two brothers started spending their lifetimes on earth, becoming the most fearsome enemies of lord Vishnu.

In their first lifetime, Jaya and Vijaya incarnated as Hiranyaksha and Hiranyakashipu, who were killed by Vishnu's incarnations lord Varaha and lord Narashimha, respectively. In their second life, they were born as Ravan and Kumbhakarna, who were killed by Rama, another incarnation of Vishnu. And in the third lifetime, they were born as Shishupala and Dantavakra. They both got killed by the most beloved incarnation of Vishnu – Krishna. After spending three lifetimes on earth, Jaya and Vijaya returned to Vaikuntha loka. They got back to performing their duties as Vishnu's gatekeepers.

2
STEALING MOTHER EARTH

There are four yugas or eras on earth – Satya Yuga, Treta Yuga, Dwapara Yuga and Kali Yuga. In Satya Yuga, there lived two asura brothers – Hiranyaksha and Hiranyakashipu, who were Jaya and Vijaya in their previous lifetime. They were cursed by the Kumara brothers to be Vishnu's enemies and hence were born on earth as asuras. Hiranyaksha was the elder one, and the king of asuras. He was evil in nature. He used to torture his subjects brutally. Gradually, he became so strong and invincible, that he defeated all the kings around the world.

Then he desired to become even more powerful than gods. As a result, his cruelty crossed all boundaries. But he knew that without having a divine boon, he would never be able to attain limitless strength. He got to know about lord Brahma, who gave boons to all those who could appease him through their conviction, inner strength and dedication! Very soon, Hiranyaksha marched to a lonely cave to start his penance, to show his reverence to Brahma. He did not eat or drink anything as he was immersed in prayer. When Brahma watched the sheer dedication of his devotee for many years, he appeared before Hiranyaksha, ready to make his wish come true by offering a boon! Seeing the lord before him,

Hiranyaksha became ecstatic and said, 'O Lord of Creation! Thank you for granting a boon to me. Kindly bless me with immortality.' Brahma was taken aback by his request. He shook his head and said, 'I can't bless you with immortality, Hiranyaksha! It is against the law of nature. One who is born, must die. It is the rule of nature. You can ask for anything else, but I cannot grant you immortality!' Hiranyaksha was lost in thoughts. After a few minutes, he said, 'Then, my lord, grant me a boon that no mortal, immortal or animal is able to kill me. I want to be invincible!'

'So be it!' Brahma nodded and went back to heaven. As soon as the lord left, Hiranyaksha laughed demonically. Now that he was all-powerful, he wanted to use his strengths to demonstrate his supremacy over the entire universe. After deep thinking, he came up with the devilish idea of kidnapping Mother Earth, who is an incarnation of Goddess Bhudevi. To implement his plan, he carried the Earth with him and dived deep into the cosmic ocean, hiding it there secretly. This caused great turmoil and chaos around the world. Seeing the turn of events, the devas panicked, thinking that this could be the end of the world. After all, how long could people and animals survive inside water?

They went to lord Vishnu to seek his help. The lord knew about Hiranyaksha's divine boon. To counter his evil intentions and outwit him, Vishnu came up with an ingenious plan. He assumed a form where his head became of a wild boar, with strong, pointed tusks. His body remained Vishnu's and the avatar came to be known as Varaha. Soon after Varaha came into existence, it went deep into the cosmic ocean, where Hiranyaksha had hidden Bhudevi. He asked him to set her free, but Hiranyaksha chuckled, shaking his head. 'I will not set her free at your whims and fancies, Varaha. You can inflict no harm to me.' Hiranyaksha knew that he was armed with Brahma's boon which ensured that he couldn't be killed by any mortal, immortal or animal.

But Varaha wasn't any ordinary god! He was half boar, half god - so technically, neither human nor god. Plus, he had massive strength to fight Hiranyaksha. As Varaha started approaching the Earth, Hiranyaksha attacked Varaha with his sword. Lord Varaha gave a severe blow on Hiranyaksha's head, sending the asura a mile off. The asura was raging with anger now. He got up to his feet again and charged at the lord! But he could hardly compete with the mighty Varaha, who shoved the asura to the ground, piercing his sharp tusks into Hiranyaksha's chest. The attack was so intense that it killed the asura instantly.

After Hiranyaksha's death, lord Varaha carried Mother Earth or Bhudevi on his tusks. He placed her back to her original position, spreading peace and harmony across the world.

3

GOD IS EVERYWHERE

When Hiranyaksha died, his younger brother, Hiranyakashipu, ascended the throne. He had witnessed how brutally Vishnu's avatar had killed his brother, so he started hating him. Just like his brother, Hiranyakashipu also desired to become the strongest of all. So he prayed to Brahma for several years. The lord was impressed and decided to grant him a wish.

When Hiranyakashipu found Brahma in front of him, he bowed earnestly, and said, 'O my lord, kindly grant me a boon that I may never be killed by any living being you created. I must not die during the daytime or at night, not inside closed doors or out in the open, neither on the ground nor in the sky. Grant me that my death not be brought by any weapon, nor by any human being or animal.'

Brahma was amazed by his desire, but since he had not asked for immortality, he did not say no. He simply fulfilled his wish. After receiving the boon, Hiranyakashipu became arrogant. He started exploiting his powers by harming innocent people.

His hatred for Vishnu was so deep-rooted that he prevented people from chanting his name and worshipping him. If his subjects were found praying to Vishnu, they were killed. Tyranny ruled everywhere, as people found no hope to live.

Hiranyakashipu had a son named Prahlad, whom he loved the most. But one day, he was stunned to see that Prahlad was chanting Vishnu's name!

He walked up to him and said, 'Son, we are asuras. We don't pray to gods like Vishnu. He is our enemy. He killed your uncle, Hiranyaksha. So, stop chanting his name.' But despite being an asura, Prahlad found great joy in chanting Vishnu's name. Seeing the unflinching devotion of his own son, infuriated Hiranyakashipu.

He was so consumed by his rage that he imprisoned Prahlad, leaving him with no food and water. But Prahlad seldom cared about anything. He continued to chant Vishnu's name dedicatedly. Everyone was astonished to see that food and water appeared magically! So, Prahlad was no longer famished.

Another time, Hiranyakashipu punished his son by putting him into a chamber full of venomous snakes. But after a while, when he swung open the door, he was irritated to see that his son was still chanting Vishnu's name, while the snakes girdled around him, tossing their heads.

He attempted several things to stop his son from praying to lord Vishnu, but all in vain. He even lost his sister in a bid to kill him – about which you will read in the next story.

At last, Hiranyakashipu became so exasperated that he decided to kill Prahlad. He tied him around a pillar of his court and growled, 'Prahlad! I will kill you this very moment. I told you to stop chanting Vishnu's name, but you didn't listen to me. Now, face your death!

But before that, tell me one thing, where is your Vishnu now? Isn't he coming to save you? Or, is he scared of me?' Prahlad calmly said, 'Father, lord Vishnu is the Supreme Lord of the Universe. Why would he be afraid of a mere asura like you? He will come to save me, for he is everywhere.

He is present in mountains, rivers, dust, flowers, even in a twig!' 'If so, then is he present in my royal palace? In this lifeless pillar?' said Hiranyakashipu, pointing to one pillar of his court Prahlad nodded with a smile. Hiranyakashipu was now provoked beyond measure. He lifted his mace, and smashed down the entire pillar to prove that his son was wrong.

And then it happened!

A bone-chilling roar shook the palace. Hiranyakashipu was dumbfounded to see that a godly being was emerging out of the broken pillar, whose face was of a fierce lion, while the rest of the body was a human's! It was Narashimha – the sixth avatar of lord Vishnu.

Hiranyakashipu's blood froze at one glimpse of the ferocious Narashimha. But he managed to say, 'So, you have come to save Prahlad from me? Don't you know that I am invincible due to

Brahma's boon? No one can harm me!' Narashimha knew about the boon. He was aware that Hiranyakashipu couldn't be killed during the day or night. But it was neither day nor night. It was the precise moment when the sun was about to go down, and twilight was about to begin.

At this very apt moment, Narasimha grabbed Hiranyakashipu by the throat, placed him right on his thigh as he wouldn't die on earth or anywhere else. He used his lion-claws as he couldn't be killed using any weapons, to tear apart the asura's stomach, bringing him to his death.

With Hiranyakashipu's death, his tyrannical rule also collapsed. Prahlad became the new asura king, spreading Vishnu's name around the world.

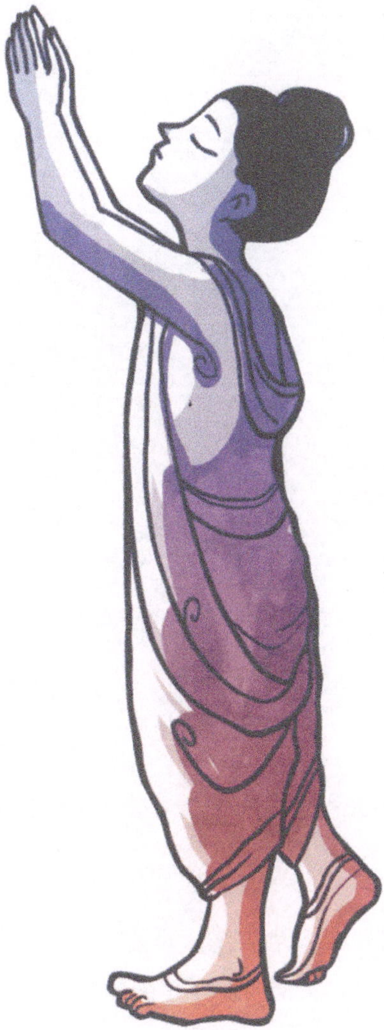

4

THE LADY DEMON

This story is about one of our favourite festivals Holi, which we celebrate every year. But surprisingly, not many people know the reason behind it.

The asura brothers – Hiranyaksha and Hiranyakashipu – had a sister, named Holika. She was hideous and used to torment people brutally. People were so petrified by her name that they did not dare to cross her path.

When Hiranyakashipu got furious about his son Prahlad's devotion towards Vishnu, he made several attempts to stop him, but failed. Until one day, when he called his sister Holika to seek her guidance and support to punish the boy.

'Brother, what do you want?' Holika asked.

Hiranyakashipu grunted in disgust, 'I want Prahlad dead. I can't bear that the boy is chanting Vishnu's name all the time!'

'Then I will make sure he is dead,' said Holika. 'I have a boon because of which fire cannot burn me down. I have a plan. Tomorrow, set a pyre where I would sit with Prahlad on my lap.

Then, you set fire around the pyre. I am fire proof, but Prahlad is not. He would burn down for sure!'

The plan seemed perfect to Hiranyakashipu. So, the very next day, he set up a pyre, where Holika sat.

As Prahlad came before Hiranyakashipu, the king ordered him to go and sit on his aunt's lap. Prahlad obeyed his father's commands. He went towards his aunt and sat on her lap. He kept chanting Vishnu's name, as always.

And right then, Hiranyakashipu set fire around the pyre. Everything started burning rapidly.

Very soon, the fire engulfed the wood, making its way up to Holika and Prahlad. But Prahlad was not agitated by the blazing fire that was surrounding him slowly. He knew that lord Vishnu was there to protect him from all kinds of evil. He simply sat in his aunt's lap, and focused on chanting.

And then, something miraculous happened!

Despite having her mighty boon, Holika started sweating a lot. She suddenly felt a burning sensation around her body, which she had never felt before. And then, she was shocked to see that her whole body was burning!

She tried to toss Prahlad aside, attempting to leap out of the pyre, but it was too late!

The fire completely engulfed everything; even Holika couldn't survive as she gave out a demonic cry, before burning down to ashes.

Now, standing at a distance, Hiranyakashipu was heartbroken and agitated looking at the events before him. He knew that his sister could not get burned by fire, but he couldn't understand why she was not saved by her boon![1] Instead, Prahlad, who was still chanting Vishnu's name, was sitting calmly, as if fire could not even touch him!

Then Prahlad said to his father, 'Whoever would chant Vishnu's name, will always be safe, for Vishnu himself is the preserver of the world.'

Hiranyakashipu grieved at his sister's death, but people around the kingdom seemed happy that Holika had fallen prey to her own devious conspiracy.

---

1. No matter how strong your boon is, it will not work if you use it to harm innocent people.

5

DEMON IN HEAVEN

Narakasura was the son of Hiranyaksha, who was as oppressive as his father. When Hiranyaksha had hidden Goddess Bhudevi under the cosmic ocean, a drop of his sweat fell on the ground. From that drop, a boy emerged, who claimed himself to be the mighty Narakasura. As he was born out of earth, Goddess Bhudevi was considered to be his mother. She was so ecstatic to have a son that she prayed to Vishnu, 'O mighty lord, grant my son such invincibility that he should only die when I wish for it.'

Vishnu blessed Narakasura as Bhudevi had wished. He also offered to him an arrow called Vaishnavastra, which could defeat even a god! When Narakasura grew up, he became the king of asuras. He built the most luxurious kingdom ever and named it Pragjyotishpura (which is now located in Guwahati). Despite all this, his asura instincts made him malicious in nature. Blinded by his invincibility, and having Vaishnavastra in hand, he decided to capture heaven to showcase his power. But he knew, it wouldn't be an easy task. To fulfil his evil ambitions, he performed sincere penance to appease Brahma. When the lord came to bless him, he said 'My lord, grant me a boon so that I can only be killed at the hands of my own mother. No one else should be able to kill me.'He knew that a mother would never kill her son. His wish came true when lord Brahma granted him the boon. Plus, his mother Bhudevi had already sought a boon that he could die only when she willed it. Now secured from both ends, Narakasura unleashed the demon inside.And then, his wickedness began!

Narakasura flew straight to heaven and fought a battle against the devas. The king of devas, Indra, defended earnestly, but he couldn't stand against Narakasura's strength. As he wielded the Vaishnavastra, Narakasura defeated Indra with ease. Indra's mother, Aditi, had a pair of celestial earrings, which were stolen by Narakasura out of spite. He also kidnapped 16,000 innocent women and imprisoned them in his palace. When Vishnu got to know about his cruelty, he told Indra, 'Narakasura's death can only happen if his mother wishes for it. But a mother would never want to kill her child. To make it happen, we will have to wait until Dwapara Yuga. I would incarnate as Krishna and bring an end to Narakasura's tyranny.'

As Dwapara Yuga arrived, Vishnu incarnated as Krishna and married Satyabhama, who was an incarnation of Bhudevi. When they got to know of Narakasura's unethical deeds, they decided to bring an end to the troubling asura. They both flew to Narakasura's palace and challenged him for a battle. Infuriated, Narakasura accepted and came to have a duel. Both, Krishna and Narakasura, fought with their sheer might. After a fierce battle, Narakasura threw the Vaishnavastra at Krishna. Unable to handle the blow, Krishna fell to the ground instantly!

Narakasura was elated that he had killed the mighty Krishna, his arch-enemy, but Satyabhama got furious. She was so enraged by the death of her husband that she immediately grabbed a trident, and hurled it towards Narakasura. The weapon flew at lightning speed and it pierced right through Narakasura's chest. He fell to the ground, wondering how Satyabhama could have killed him when it could only be done by his mother, Bhudevi! Right then, Krishna sprang to his feet, startling everyone. Satyabhama was bewildered upon seeing the turn of events. She asked, 'Oh dear husband, I thought you were dead!' Krishna smiled and said, 'I was pretending to be dead because I knew only you could kill Narakasura. You are the incarnation of Bhudevi, who is Narakasura's mother.'

Narakasura realized it was Krishna's trick before he succumbed to death. Krishna and Satyabhama freed all the 16,000 women who were trapped by Narakasura. Then, they went to Dwarka, their home. When Krishna and Satyabhama returned, it was a moonless night. The people of Dwarka were ecstatic as their lord had triumphed over evil. To graciously welcome him, they cleaned their houses and streets. They lit lamps as a symbol to celebrate his victory. Soon, the entire city was illuminating with colourful lights as people were delighted to have Krishna back. Eventually, this celebration was called Diwali which is one of the most important Hindu festivals. It is celebrated every year with immense joy and enthusiasm.[2]

---

2. Diwali is also described as a homecoming celebration of Rama, Lakshmana and Sita in the Ramayana.

6

HOW TO DECEIVE AN ASURA

Mura was the supreme commander of Narakasura's army of asuras. He was in charge of Pragjyotishpura's protection. Being an asura, Mura was strong and well-built. He was almost as powerful as Narakasura himself. But after Narakasura's death, he realized that asuras could never stand against the force of devas. That thought made him sceptical about his own strength. He resolved to become more powerful than devas so that no one could ever defeat him. Thus, he prayed to Brahma for a boon, which could earn him limitless strength.When Brahma appeared in front of him, Mura said, 'My lord, grant me a boon so that in any battle, if I touch someone, the person dies instantly - irrespective of whether they are gods or mortals.' Soon after Brahma granted him the boon, the asura marched towards heaven and started battling with Indra. The king of devas couldn't defend himself from Mura's attack. Therefore, he retreated, leaving heaven under Mura's rule.

For a long time, Mura held heaven under his rule. Until his eyes fell on Yama – the God of Death. Mura knew, if he could ever defeat Yama, he would become immortal! He attacked Yama instantly. He was so powerful that the God of Death had no choice but to accept defeat. No god in heaven dared to face Mura's strength, as he had Brahma's mighty boon. So, the asura kept ruling over heaven, without any fear. When everyone reached Brahma and begged for a solution, he said, 'I gave him this boon because I was impressed by his devotion. But now, I don't know how to control him! He could never be killed by employing strength. Rather, he could only be outwitted by a clever trick. Who could be better than the witty Krishna to defeat him? Only he can outwit the asura!'

After listening to these words, the entourage of gods reached Krishna. They explained everything about the misery that was caused by Mura. Krishna passed a serene smile upon hearing of their troubles. He pacified them and said, 'That won't be a hard task for me! I will go and see what Mura can do to me.' Then, Krishna invited Mura to meet him at the sea shore. Mura became sceptical upon receiving his invite. He knew that Krishna was a very witty god. He wondered whether it was a trap! 'But who can trap me, the mighty Mura, who has defeated every god in heaven!'

Consumed by his overconfidence, he went to meet Krishna. When he reached the seashore, he asked, 'O Krishna, why did you call me?' Krishna smiled cunningly and said, 'Mura, I have heard that you are so powerful that even the gods are afraid to face you! Is that true?' Mura laughed at Krishna's compliment. 'That is true, Krishna. They are so fearful of me that they never dare to face my strength! But why on earth did you come here to meet me? Don't you know, if I want, I can even kill you!' Krishna said, 'I am here exactly for this reason. I want to fight with you. Let's see, who is stronger?'

Mura let out a demonic laugh, and said, 'You don't know me, Krishna. If I touch anyone in the battlefield, that person would die instantly! You will also die if you fight with me!' 'I didn't know that! I should have known it before I challenged you. Now see, I am so petrified. My hands and limbs are trembling. I can hear my heart throbbing out of fear! Surprisingly, I can hear your heartbeat, too. Are you getting scared of me?' 'Why would I get afraid of you?' Mura demanded. 'Actually, I can hear everything from a mile away. Along with my own heart, I can hear the rapid movement of your heart . You are so terrified!' said Krishna, with a laugh.

Mura protested, 'It is not true! I am not afraid of you. My heart isn't pounding out of fear!' And then, to prove Krishna wrong, he touched his heart. Just as suddenly, Brahma's boon came into effect. And before Mura could comprehend the entire matter, he fell at Krishna's feet, dead.

Krishna laughed out loud and said, 'You are not supposed to touch anyone, Mura. Not even your heart! See what you have done to yourself!' Then, Krishna gave the heaven to gods and peace prevailed. Later, Krishna also came to be known as Murari – the slayer of Mura.

7

THE MOST GENEROUS ASURA THAT EVER LIVED

Not all asuras were wicked, desiring to rule over heaven unethically. There were some who got so prosperous that they were praised like gods. One of them was king Bali. He was the son of Virochana, grandson of Prahlad. Like his grandfather, Bali was also a great devotee of lord Vishnu. He had a heart full of generosity. Despite being an asura, he was kind to his subjects. He became a benevolent ruler, who ruled his kingdom righteously. In his reign, everyone was happy and prosperous. People revered him like a god. Bali had learned his lessons from Guru Shukracharya, who was one of the mighty sages. He taught him the knowledge of Vedas. Once Bali acquired his education, he grew so powerful that he defeated Indra, the king of heaven. It was a perfect opportunity for him to rule over heaven. But Bali wasn't like other asuras. Although he conquered the whole heaven, he didn't capture it. He bowed to Indra and handed it to him. One day, guru Sukracharya told him, 'Bali, you are immensely powerful. You can easily become the lord of heaven, earth and hell. But for that, you will have to perform a hundred Ashwamedha yajnas. I say, you must perform it.' Instantly, Bali acted upon his guru's words. He started his preparation in full swing, and the Ashwamedha yajna started.Meanwhile, in heaven, Indra got scared of Bali's yajna. He thought that the asura might have a change of heart someday. He may become wicked and malicious. He knew that Bali couldn't do evil things, but still, his heart wasn't at peace.

He went to Vishnu and complained, 'My lord, please stop Bali right at this very moment! If he completes the yajna, he could be invincible. And then, no god would be able to defeat him!' Vishnu smiled and said, 'Indra, don't be so worried about Bali. He is my devotee. I know his heart is in the right place! He is certainly an asura. But you should not forget that he is the grandson of Prahlad, who was also an asura, but my dear devotee. I assure you that you should not be fearful of Bali.' But Vishnu's words did not comfort him. He requested, 'My lord, I know Bali is one of your great devotees, but being the king of heaven, I am concerned about its safety. I request you on behalf of all the devas, do something about Bali. I am not telling you to kill the asura right away, but I am requesting you to do something so that heaven can be safe even if he stays alive.'

Now, Vishnu was perplexed. He knew that Bali would never take any step against the gods. Still, being the preserver of the universe, he had to act on Indra's concern. He came up with a plan. He incarnated as lord Vamana – a dwarf brahmin, and walked straight to Bali's kingdom where he found Bali to be completing his Ashwamedha yajna. Bali was offering alms to the brahmins when he reached. When Bali saw the dwarf brahmin, he asked for his identity.Vamana said, 'My name is Vamana and I am here to seek something from you. I have heard that you are a generous king. I want to see your kindness. Can you give me whatever I want?' 'I am a king,' said Bali. 'And I can give you anything you want. Wealth, food, shelter – anything that might please you!' said Bali. He thought that a mere dwarf brahmin wouldn't ask for something valuable. He did not know that the dwarf was Vishnu! 'I only want as much land as I can cover in three footsteps.'

Bali was startled, looking at the brahmin's little legs that could hardly cover a metre. But Sukracharya, his guru, sensed something odd about the brahmin.

He told Bali not to offer anything. But denying the request of the brahmin would be a sin. A generous king like Bali could never commit that sin! So he nodded at Vamana, and said, 'Oh respected one, take the land as you have asked for.' And then Vamana expanded his size so enormously that his head almost reached the sky. His whole figure covered the earth, as he said, 'I put my first step on earth, so it is mine.' After that, he stretched his second leg, way up to the sky, saying, 'I put my second step towards the sky, so it is mine.'

Now, Bali understood that Vamana was no ordinary dwarf. He folded his hands and asked, 'O great one, you have taken the earth and heaven. Now, kindly place your third step on my head. I have nothing to offer you but myself!' And then, a third leg appeared out of Vamana's belly-button, as he placed it on Bali's head. The asura king asked Vamana to show his real form. When the brahmin showed his real identity, he said, 'I am pleased with your devotion and kindness, Bali. From this day, you will be known as Mahabali.I am sending you to the underworld, where you will rule as the king. And now, you can ask for anything you want.'

'I want nothing, my lord,' said Bali, seeing his lord in front of him. 'I only want to return to my kingdom once every year, to ensure that my people are leading a happy life.' 'So be it!' Vishnu granted as he pushed Bali to the underworld.

And from then on, every year, Mahabali used to return for one day to his kingdom, which was in Kerala. People started celebrating their king's homecoming as a festival named Onam, where they decorated their houses with colourful lamps. Gifts were exchanged and feasts were held everywhere.

8

TRAP A GOD FOR PROTECTION

Banasura was the eldest son of Bali. He was a great devotee of Shiva. Through his long penance, he managed to please Shiva, who blessed him with one thousand arms. But Banasura was seeking something else, as he said, 'My lord, if you are really impressed with my devotion, kindly be my protector. Promise to protect me all the time.' Shiva accepted his wish and blessed him. But Banasura was hardly going to use his boon for a good purpose. With time, he became wicked. He went across the world, wreaking havoc and chaos in all the kingdoms. And no one dared to face the one thousand-armed Banasura, whose protector was Shiva himself!

His boon made him so impulsive that he charged into Shiva's abode, Kailash. He demolished everything that came in his way. Shiva grew so angry that he wished to cut off Banasura's head, but he had promised the asura for protection, so he could do nothing. But he warned, 'With the breaking of your palace-flagpole, your nuisance shall end for sure!'

But Banasura did not get bothered by Shiva's words, as he was convinced that the lord himself was at his protection. Banasura had a daughter named Usha, who was very beautiful. One day, Usha dreamt of a prince. He was so charming and handsome that she fell in love with him. And at the break of her dream, she desired to marry him. So, she called Chitralekha, her handmaiden, who knew black magic. She told her about the dream. Using her dark tricks, Chitralekha painted a portrait of the same prince Usha had dreamt of. Then she said, 'His name is Aniruddha. He is the grandson of lord Krishna!' Despite being the daughter of an asura, Usha desperately wished to marry him. So Chitralekha travelled to Dwarka, disguising as a woman. She abducted Aniruddha and brought him to the princess. When Aniruddha got to his senses, Usha explained her dream to him. The prince agreed to marry her, as he was also charmed by her beauty.

Banasura was unaware of this event, until his eyes fell on his palace-flagpole, which was now tilted. When he came to know of Aniruddha's presence in the palace, he was immediately reminded of Shiva's warning. Getting enraged by his daughter's deed, Banasura dashed to Usha's chamber, only to find Aniruddha with her. He imprisoned the prince in a cell. To ensure that no one can set him free, he doubled the guard around the cell. Meanwhile, in Dwarka, the news of Aniruddha's abduction spread like wildfire. When Krishna got to know that Banasura had captured his grandson, he was filled with rage. He marched to Banasura's palace with his brother, Balarama. Krishna knew Banasura wouldn't release Aniruddha so easily, so he demanded a battle with the asura. Before it began, Shiva had to appear to protect the asura. Krishna pleaded Shiva to move away, but Shiva couldn't help it. He had promised the asura for protection. So Krishna had to fight with Shiva. The duo fought like two mighty warriors. Shiva hurled multiple divine weapons, but nothing could harm Krishna. He defended Shiva's attacks effortlessly. He was even ready to use the Sudarshana Chakra, when Shiva got ready with his divine Trident. But before the two supreme weapons could collide, Krishna realized that Shiva was protecting Banasura as he had promised to save him. He did not have any affinity with the asura. Rather, he was just keeping his word.

And thus, to save Shiva, Krishna plotted a plan.He shot a miraculous arrow at Shiva, which made the lord fall to the ground. He was not dead, but unconscious. As soon as Shiva fell into a deep slumber, Banasura lost his sole protection. At this very apt moment, Krishna used his Sudarshana Chakra to chop Banasura's arms. He was about to kill the asura when Shiva woke up from his slumber. He pleaded to Krishna to absolve Banasura's sin as he was his devotee.Krishna heard Shiva's words and instead of killing the asura, he released him. Banasura also felt sorry for imprisoning Krishna's grandson. Soon, he freed Aniruddha and agreed to marrying his daughter Usha to Aniruddha.

Krishna felt ecstatic at this event as the wedding happened with a lot of cheer and happiness.

9

GOD OF WAR

Sati, the first consort of Shiva, was so dear to the lord that she became a part of him. When she died, Shiva grew so remorseful that he vowed never to marry again. Leaving everything behind, he went to Kailash mountain, where he started meditating in a lonely cave. When a terrible asura named Tarakasura learnt about Shiva's vow, he decided to do something wicked.

Tarakasura desired to become the king of heaven so that people could worship him like devas. But he knew, for such accomplishment, he needed a boon that could make him invincible like the other gods. Thus, he performed austerities to please Brahma. When the lord appeared, the asura said, 'My lord, grant me a boon so that I could only be killed by Shiva's son.'

It was such a strange desire that Brahma was astonished. And Tarakasura knew that Shiva had vowed never to marry again, so he wouldn't have a son. After all, Shiva would never break his vow! After getting this boon, Tarakasura became arrogant as he started raising an army of asuras. Once he was ready, he went to heaven and challenged Indra for a battle.

Indra also gathered his army of devas to protect their home - heaven. Along with Agni – the god of fire, Varun – the god of water and Yama – the god of death, he started fighting Tarakasura.

The battle went on for days, but the devas couldn't stand against the army of asuras. No one was able to kill Tarakasura and attain victory.

After being defeated, the devas then retreated from heaven and sought the help of Brahma.

Brahma, however, couldn't find any idea to help the devas. So, everyone flew to Shiva – the Destroyer. They pleaded with him to do something to stop the asura.

But Shiva remained stuck to his vow. They realized that as long as Shiva did not marry, his son wouldn't be born. Till then, the gods will have to suffer the torment of asuras.

Finding no way out, the entourage of devas prayed to Shakti – the Goddess of the Universe. They described their miserable situation caused by Tarakasura.

Goddess Shakti felt pity on the condition of the devas, so she decided to help them. Then she incarnated as Parvati and went to Kailash. She tried to convince Shiva to marry her.

Shiva, however, denied Parvati's proposal and continued with his meditation. But Parvati was adamant! She also started meditating.

Gradually, Shiva realized that she was none other than his Sati. It was her second life.

Due to this realization, Shiva accepted Parvati's marriage proposal and they got married. Very soon, they had a son named Kartikeya, who was resplendent like a thousand suns.

Kartikeya grew up rather quickly, not taking long years like you and me. When he came to know that he was destined to kill Tarakasura, he brought together the army of gods. Wielding his long spear, he marched to wipe out the asura.

As soon as Tarakasura got a glimpse of Kartikeya, he got ready for battle. But no matter how much he tried to oppose Shiva's son, he just couldn't do it.

Tarakasura flung several weapons, but Kartikeya defended himself effortlessly. And then, raising his spear, Kartikeya pierced the weapon right through the asura's chest. That was the end of Tarakasura.

Thus, Tarakausra's evil attempts ended and everyone hailed Kartikeya as 'The God of War'.

10

THE UNBEATABLE ASURA

A long time ago, there lived an asura named Gajamukhasura, who was so strong that everyone used to be scared of him. No one dared to face his wrath. And men used to get dubious about their own strength before the asura, and kept avoiding his way. Gajamukhasura knew he would remain dreadful to human beings, as they were fragile and weak. But he also knew that gods could easily defeat him, as they were more powerful than him. He did not want that to happen.

Being an ardent worshipper of lord Shiva, Gajamukhasura made up his mind to perform a long penance to appease the lord. He knew that if he was successful, lord Shiva would definitely grant him a boon. And with that boon, he could rule the world, even heaven! As his asura-brain was convinced about his evil plan, he made his way to a dense forest, and started meditating to please Shiva. Months and years passed, but Gajamukhasura remained firm in his resolve. Whether it was winter, summer or rainy season around him, he kept chanting Shiva's name. Now, Shiva is an affectionate and kind god who never discriminated between his devotees. When he saw Gajamukhasura praying to him with so much of dedication, he found his heart melting. So he decided to appear before the asura.

When he appeared before Gajamukhasura, the asura felt ecstatic. He said, 'My lord, you have come, at last!' 'I am pleased with your devotion, Gajamukhasura. How can I hold myself back if my devotee is praying to me so sincerely?' 'I am delighted to see you, my lord,' said Gajamukhasura, bowing deeply. Shiva nodded. 'I am so pleased with your prayer that I shall bless you with a boon! Tell me, what do you seek?' 'Oh god, I have only one desire. Kindly grant me a boon that I always remain far from death. No weapon should ever be the cause of my death.' He was so sure of his physical prowess that he was sure that protection against weapons will be a good plan. Shiva nodded. 'Whatever you wish for, Gajamukhasura!'

After getting the boon, Gajamukhasura became more powerful. He thought he was deathless! Then he sauntered from kingdom to kingdom and captured those lands, defeating all the kings. Human beings started getting afraid of Gajamukhasura's might. They tried to be as away from him as possible. He forced everyone to chant his name as their ultimate lord and prevented everyone from praying to the Trinity. If they were found chanting anyone else's name, they would get killed in no time!

When the gods got to know about Gajamukhasura's mean acts, they rushed to Shiva, seeking his help. But Shiva said, 'I can't defeat this asura on my own. I have given him the boon that no weapon can kill him.' 'But you must do something to stop his wicked acts, my lord,' chorused all the gods.

After a brief moment, Shiva called his son, Ganesha. Ganesha is the elephant-headed god, who is chiefly famous for his unbeatable wit and sheer strength. He is very dutiful towards his parents.

When Ganesha appeared before Shiva, he got to know about Gajamukhasura's acts of terror. 'Father, I would love to help defeat the asura.' Knowing fully well that he would be the right person for the task, Shiva and other gods bade Ganesha goodbye. As soon as Gajamukhasura found Ganesha before him, the asura chuckled deceitfully and said, 'O Ganesha, don't you know, I am immortal! Why are you carrying so many weapons? To kill me?' Then he laughed the loudest. 'Don't you know, your father has given me a boon of protection against all weapons!' But Ganesha didn't care about Gajamukhasura's words. He wielded his mace and landed a heavy blow on the asura's head. Instead of dying instantly, or even getting upset with the blow, Ganesha was stunned to find Gajamukhasura laughing!

Then he shot hundreds of arrows, but it did not bother the asura even one bit. Ganesha attempted every possible way to bring about the asura's death, but Gajamukhasura didn't as much as move. He remained as strong as ever. Now, Ganesha was sure - Gajamukhasura wouldn't die of any weapon. So he decided to use his mind. He dropped all his weapons and pretended that he was tired of this fight.

Gajamukhasura couldn't understand Ganesha's trick. He was a master of stealth, and could change his form at will. So he changed himself into a tiny mouse and scurried towards Ganesha, wishing to startle the lord for fun. But Ganesha was witty enough. As soon as the mouse came closer, he leapt in the air and plopped down on its back!

Ganesha's weight was too much for that tiny mouse as he couldn't tolerate his weight on its back. Soon, it gave in and apologized, 'O Ganesha, let me go, or else I will die!' Ganesha chuckled and said, 'I will only release you if you promise that you will become my devotee and my divine carrier.' Gajamukhasura had no way out. He nodded and agreed to Ganesha's proposal.

And from that day on, the invincible Gajamukhasura became Ganesha's devotee and his carrier – the mouse.

11

HOW TO SEPARATE THE INSEPARABLE

In times of yore, there lived two daunting and mischievous asura brothers – Sunda and Upasunda. They were inseparable and could read each other's thoughts. They shared their food, drinks, clothes and even the kingdom. They had everything to lead a lavish and comfortable life, but their asura natre messed with their minds. Despite having so much, they couldn't ignore their greed for more. In their quest for becoming unconquerable, they performed austerities to appease Brahma and get the desired boons.Their sincere penance impressed Brahma and he appeared. The brothers sought to become immortal. But Brahma was very strict about this desire and made it clear that he would never grant them a boon that was against the law of nature!So he shook his head and told them that immortality could never be granted. They had to think of something else. Denied their top demand, and given a second chance, the brothers discussed and said, 'My lord, if you can't bless us with immortality, then grant us such a boon that we die only at the hands of each other, and by no one else!' They had asked for such a boon, overconfident that they would never get into any fight - ever! But Brahma knew better. He had seen enough asuras abuse their boons to harm people and gods. Now, every time he granted a boon, he wove in some loophole, leaving a scope to stop the asuras, if the need so arose. Now, as the brothers had wished, Brahma granted them the boon, but he also wove a loophole, before bidding them goodbye.

Very soon, the brothers started misusing their boon, as expected. On a whim, they dashed into different kingdoms and wreaked havoc. They laid their hands on the thrones and kicked the kings away from their kingdoms. Their subjects were tormented, families tortured and there was a lot of chaos everywhere. Their evil acts were spreading like wildfire and everyone prayed to Brahma, seeking his help. Brahma knew this would happen, sooner or later. So he was more prepared to handle it this time. He told the gods, 'You need not worry about them, for their time has come. They will now have to pay for all their deeds!' As the gods watched, Brahma sculpted a beautiful enchantress, naming her Tilottama. The gods were mesmerised as he breathed life into her. Her beauty captivated even the devas, which made Brahma confident that this plan would work.

One day, when Sunda and Upasunda were strolling in their kingdom, taking regular update about the work, they got a glimpse of Tilottama. One look at her and they were charmed by her beauty! They kept gazing at her, until Sunda said, 'I must marry this beauty!' Upasunda, who was also equally enamoured with Tilottama's beauty, snorted at his brother's statement and said, 'No, not you. I'm going to marry her!'

Sunda jerked his head. 'Stop ranting, brother! I'm your elder and I've got the right to marry her. She is your sister-in-law!' Upasunda didn't like Sunda's comment. He grumbled, 'It doesn't matter whether you are elder or not! I saw her first, so technically, I have the first and only right to marry her.' They kept grumbling about the matter, but then decided to handle the matter calmly. They decided to walk over to her and ask her who she would want to marry. They were brothers, after all, and would honour this rule. Tilottama saw the two brothers approaching, and geared up for the plan. The brothers updated her about their desire. She smiled her enchanted smile and said, 'I have vowed to marry the strongest man in the world. So whoever is stronger out of the two of you, I shall marry him. Now you better decide yourselves, who is stronger!'

The brothers looked at each other and smiled, each thinking he was stronger than the other. Also secretly hoping that the other would back down.Finally, they decided to have a duel, and the winner would marry Tilottama. But see, how foolish they really were! Till moments ago, they were inseparable at any cost. The next, because of a girl, they started battling like enraged bulls, forgetting their boon. They fought furiously and the ground shook. And by the end of their fight, they killed each other with their own hands, getting nothing fruitful at all.

Everyone in the world was relived with the death of the asura brothers. They would finally be free of two cruel rulers. All this while, Brahma chuckled and said, 'What can't be achieved by battle, can easily be achieved by beauty!'

12

INDRA'S FEAR

Vritrasura was a name that invoked terror in the hearts of gods and humans alike. He had almost ruined the life of Indra, the king of heaven. He was such a powerful asura that his name was enough to scare anyone. Armed with a boon to never be killed by any weapon made of metal or wood, he wreaked havoc over all the three worlds[3]. Like all his other demon friends, he became arrogant once he had acquired the boon. And now he desired to capture heaven - the gorgeous home to the devas. Capturing heaven wasn't an easy task! So he started gathering a massive army of asuras and declared, 'My asura brothers, we are suffering on this earth, squirming like worms. Look at the devas! They are enjoying their life, drinking nectar and ruling over us! Don't you think that pleasure should be ours? Let's charge at heaven and drive the devas out! Then it will be all ours.'

Everyone agreed with their leader's words and started preparing for the battle. They were keeping a watch over the devas. Then one day, when the asuras noticed that the devas were busy enjoying their blissful life, they attacked swarga lok - heaven.

---

3. The heaven, earth and hell.

The devas were startled with the sudden attack and couldn't withstand it. Indra, however, fought very hard. In the end, he was defeated and had to run away to save his life. He realised that no weapon was having any effect on Vritrasura. What was this happening? The devas retreated unwillingly, leaving heaven in Vritrasura's hand. After this great defeat, the devas rushed to Brahma. They wanted to find a way out to defeat the asura army. Brahma told them, 'Vritrasura can't be killed, for he has such a boon that weapons made of metal or wood could never kill him.' 'Does that mean heaven will suffer under him forever? There should be an alternate. Tell us how we can defeat him,' Indra pleaded desperately.

Brahma smiled back and said, 'Yes, there is only one way, though it is not going to be easy. Indra, you will have to go to the earth. There is a sage named Dadhichi. By long meditation and austerities, he has gained celestial strength in his bones. Go to him and try to get his bones! You can use them against Vritrasura.' 'Bones!' Indra grew sceptical. 'Yes, bones,' said Brahma. 'If he agrees to offer you his bones, then with the help of Vishwakarma[4], you can create a weapon that can be Virtrasura's end.'

Seeing a ray of hope in the otherwise gloomy situation, Indra, along with the other devas, soon reached the cottage of sage Dadhichi. The sage was truly bewildered, finding the devas at his doorstep. Imagine all the gods coming to see you! Wouldn't it baffle you too? He asked the devas what the matter was. Indra paid his respects to the sage by bowing down and then described their

---

4. A craftsman deity; also the divine architect of the devas.

miserable situation.

'We sought the help of Brahma,' said Indra, 'but he also couldn't help us. He is the one who advised us to come to you. He told us that your penance has given your bones remarkable strength. And if you can give us your bones, we can use it to produce a weapon to defeat the demon. That is why we are here, to seek your help. Would you kindly help the devas?' Being a kind sage, Dadhichi realized the miserable situation of the devas and sympathized with them. He also agreed to offer his bones to them. Dahichi said, 'I know, giving you my bones would mean death for me. But not many people get a chance to die for the gods, to be of help to them. Besides, if Brahma has suggested this, and if my bones can bring you victory over evil, I will most humbly help!' Then, the mighty sage sat in meditation and uttered something under his breath.

Very soon, there rose a great fire around the sage's body. Moments later, the sage burned himself down for the gods. But everyone present there was amazed to see that his bones hadn't caught fire! Indra then meticulously collected the bones and took them to Vishwakarma.

Vishwakarma was the divine engineer of the gods, and when he heard everything from Indra, he promptly produced a mighty weapon out of Dadhichi's spine.'Here,' he said. 'This weapon is called Vajra. It would release thunderbolts at its waving. It certainly would bring Vritrasura's end.'Wielding the Vajra, Indra then gathered all the devas and waged battle against Vritrasura.

Vritrasura, however, was not aware of the Vajra, and what it was made of. It was the devas' secret weapon against the evil asura. Vritrasura, high on confidence, assumed that he would defeat Indra – this time too!But how wrong he was! Very soon, the devas and asuras started battling against each other, and no one dared to kill Vritrasura. His boon repelled every strike over him.

When the asuras started overpowering the devas, Indra entered into the battleground, riding his giant white elephant – Airavat. Without losing any time, he fished out his Vajra, and waved it in the air. Thousands of thunderbolts cracked out from its tip and rained down heavily over the asuras, reducing them to ashes. Vritrasura panicked at seeing this new weapon and its power. In a rage, he charged at Indra. But it was too late!

Indra shot another thunderbolt and it pierced right across Vritrasura's chest, turning him into ashes as well. With Vritrasura's death, the asuras were defeated. Some were killed, some wounded, and others fled from the battlefield.

The devas took over heaven once again, spreading peace everywhere.

13

UNDERNEATH THE OCEAN

Kalakeya was the commander-in-chief of Vritrasura's army of asuras. When Indra killed Vritrasura by shooting thunderbolts from his Vajra, a few asuras fled from the battlefield and dived deep into the great ocean. They were scared of Indra's fury and wanted to save their lives. Kalakeya was one of them. He wanted to get the army of asuras back again, to create chaos in the world, to irritate the devas. He suggested that all asuras must live underneath the ocean. They were not like humans, so they could live under water with ease. There, they lived for long, cursing Indra and waiting for a chance to take revenge.

One day, Kalakeya came up with a plan. He gathered the asuras and said, 'My asura brothers! You all know, how Indra had defeated us and killed our leader, Vritrasura. But now, we will avenge his death. Time has come to do something horrific. It is now time to turn the blissful lives of gods into a terrible curse!' Everyone agreed with Kalakeya and asked him how they could achieve such a thing!

Kalakeya said, 'We can achieve this by killing the sages on earth! They claim to be the true devotees of gods. If we start harming them one by one, they would pray to the gods for protection. But the gods will never find us and then the humans will be more devoted to us! We will go back into hiding underneath the ocean after we have killed. The ocean is vast, limitless, and the devas would never find us!'

As they had planned, the asuras started creeping out of the ocean every night. Using the cover of darkness, they started killing the sages and their kin one by one. Then, they crawled back into the ocean again, without anybody knowing who was responsible for all the bloodshed. This horrific events went on for days, until the sages prayed to lord Indra for help. Indra was perplexed to know this and came down to help the sages at once. It did not take him too long to figure out what was happening. He was the king of gods, after all. He knew Kalakeya was behind all this. But Indra also knew he would never be able to find them under the ocean. He would need help to find where exactly they were hidden beneath the layers of water. So, Indra reached out to Brahma to seek help. Brahma said, 'Until Kalakeya remains hidden underneath the ocean, you can never defeat him. So find a way to bring him out!'

Indra confessed that this was a well-thought out plan by the asuras and no temptation would bring them out. Brahma added, 'But what if you can somehow dry up the whole ocean? Then you can surely finish them off!' 'But how can we ever dry the whole ocean?' asked Indra, dazed. 'The ocean is limitless. Where would all the water go? How can anyone dry it?' 'I know someone who can do it with ease,' said Brahma. Indra was mighty impressed as Brahma told him, 'Reach out to sage Agastya and tell him about the miserable situation the other sages are in. He will definitely help you.'

So the very next day, the devas reached sage Agastya and described how Kalakeya was torturing and killing so many. Being a sage himself, Agastya could understand the terrible pain it was to lose such learned members. So he agreed to help the gods at once. He said, 'Don't worry. I will drink the whole ocean for you, and you can find Kalakeya and the other asuras.' Indra had never thought a sage could drink the whole ocean! But at the same time, he couldn't doubt Brahma's words. He quickly brought the sage to the ocean shore and watched. Sage Agastya walked into the water till his knees were immersed in it. He bent forth and started drinking. He sipped and sipped and gradually, the water level started going down. Everyone was bewildered at seeing the sage drink up the ocean with such ease! While the gods were surprised, it seemed like an easy task for Agastya.

Where the ocean water was touching them moments ago, there now remained no glimpse of water anywhere. Only the earth and sand could be seen as far as you stretched your vision. With that, the gods could see Kalakeya and a group of asuras huddling at a distance. They were as amazed at the drying up of the ocean as the others. It was like the ocean had suddenly vanished! Then the asuras got a glimpse of Indra, and their hearts started throbbing in fear.

Indra didn't waste a minute after that. He pulled his Vajra out, and with one swing, released thousands of thunderbolts over the asuras.None of the asuras were quick enough to escape or hide. Everyone, including Kalakeya, was reduced to ashes.The gods then celebrated the death of those who had killed so many noble sages in the past few days. They thanked sage Agastya for his help.

Many years later, king Bhagiratha – the grandson of king Sagar – pleased goddess Ganga with his devotion and brought Ganga down to the earth. That is how the dried ground was filled with water once again

14

EMERGING OUT OF EARWAX

There was once a time when our world was fully immersed in cosmic waters. There were no humans, no animals, no plants and not even soil on our earth. Wherever you would look, you would find endless water. Only Brahma, the Creator of the world, would sit on a celestial lotus, and lord Vishnu used to lie down on the giant multi-headed snake, Adi-Shesha.

This was the time when the creation of the world had just begun. And that is when this current story takes place. One day, Vishnu was taking a nap on his snake-bed. In a restful state, two drops of his earwax fell into the ocean. What happened next was almost unbelievable! From the two drops emerged two huge asuras. They claimed to be Madhu and Kaitabha.

But they looked around, wondering where they were and what they were doing in the middle of vast waters! They wanted answers, but there was nobody to guide them. So they decided to meditate on god and performed penance for long years. In the end, goddess Shakti appeared before them. She told them about their birth and was pleased with their penance. She wanted to grant them a boon for their sincerity in meditation. Madhu and Kaitabha were too overwhelmed to know so much about their birth. And on top of it, this boon! They somehow managed to say, 'If you really were pleased with our devotion, then bless us that we shall only die when we so wish.''So be it,' blessed the goddess before she turned to vanish.

The asuras looked at each other, wondering what had just happened. Madhu said, 'I don't understand what happened? What did she mean by the boon?

''She was happy that we spent time in penance, and thus blessed us with a boon. Now we will only die when we wish to. Till then, we can live without fear and do whatever we wish to!' said Kaitabha with a cunning smile.

They started roaming the cosmic ocean and found a great divine lotus. Lord Brahma sat on it peacefully, chanting the Vedas. The asuras smiled at each other and charged at Brahma to test their prowess.Reaching over to the lord, the asuras started tormenting Brahma and attempted to snatch the Vedas.

When the lord refused, the asuras tried to kill him. Feeling helpless, Brahma flung himself out of the lotus and scampered towards Vishnu, hoping to get help.

That is how Vishnu learned about his nap, and how the notorious asuras had emerged from his earwax. He also got to know about the boon granted by Shakti, but still promised Brahma that he would take care of it. Chasing Brahma, Madhu and Kaitabha also reached the abode of Vishnu. There they saw Vishnu ready with his mace and Sudarshana Chakra to fight them.There started a great battle between Vishnu and the asuras.Both sides fought very hard, but no matter how much Vishnu tried to oppose and kill the asuras, Madhu and Kaitabha remained unharmed.

Vishnu tried several times, but every time he tried to smash the asuras, they would be fine the next moment. He just could not kill them.Vishnu then realized that Madhu and Kaitabha would only die when they would wish to – thanks to the boon by goddess Shakti. Vishnu prayed to the goddess, asking for a way out. He had to wipe out the mean asuras and save Brahma, at any cost. 'You can't kill them by your might,' said the goddess. 'To wipe them out, you will have to trick them!'

Vishnu nodded, and turning to Madhu and Kaitabha, he said, 'I am mighty impressed with your power. I am also pleased with your battle skills and strategies. See, I am a god and I would like to grant you a boon. Ask me anything you want.' The asuras laughed mockingly, and with arrogance, they said, 'You are unable to defeat us, and now you want to bless us? How funny is that! We are mightier than you and you know it. So let's do this! You ask for a boon and we will be happy to grant it to you!'

Vishnu had been waiting for just this chance. He said, 'If you really want to grant me a boon, then I wish you to get killed by me!' Madhu and Kaitabha shuddered at this desire of the lord. They had never thought Vishnu would ask for such a thing! They also knew that since they had promised to grant any boon, they would now have to fulfil it.

Sadly, knowing that it would mean their end, they nodded, 'So be it!' But they also put a condition. 'But on the condition that we will only die on land, not in this ocean.' How smart! There was no sort of land around the world – only ocean and ocean wherever you could see.

But nothing is impossible for the mighty Vishnu! He simply stretched his thigh on the ocean and produced a surface, just like land. He then ordered the asuras to place their heads on his stretched thigh. The asuras accepted defeat and placed their heads on Vishnu's thigh. The Lord beheaded them with his mighty Sudarshana Chakra.

The fat or 'meda' from their bodies filled the earth and created the earthly ground. That is why the earth is also called 'Medini.'

15

THE TERRIBLE BOON

Bhasmasura was an asura who desired to become the most powerful in the world. He wanted everyone to fear him, so that no one could ever challenge him. But he didn't know how to achieve such strength. One day, while strolling on the earth, he came face to face with the celestial sage, Narada.

Narada was the son of Brahma, who was renowned as the mischief-maker. He is someone who knows a lot, but troubles everyone for his entertainment. He is not evil, just naughty like some young children. He is also very talented. He can travel to different realms, playing his tambura *(a stringed musical instrument)* and chanting Vishnu's name. He also serves as the connection between gods and humans; heaven and earth.

Bhasmasura was aware of the fact that Narada knew everything. Nothing could get hidden from the sage. So, he decided to use this opportunity for his gain.

He bowed his head and asked, 'O sage Narada, you know everything. You can help me with good advice. There is nobody else in this world who can help me, I know.'

With such praise, Narada was quite happy. So he asked Bhasmasura what he wanted to know. 'I want to become the most powerful of all. How can I fulfil my heart's desire?' Bhasmasura asked.

Narada smiled and said, 'O Bhasmasura, you must perform severe penance to please Lord Shiva. Not only is he easy to please with true devotion, but also powerful enough to grant you such a boon.' So, the very next day, Bhasmasura went deep into the forest and started meditating on Shiva. After years of penance, Shiva was happy with Bhasmasura's devotion and couldn't hold himself back from seeing him.

Shiva appeared in front of Bhasmasura, to meet his devotee in person. The asura got excited on seeing the lord and said, 'My lord, you have come! I was waiting for you. Please grant me a boon.' Shiva smiled and nodded at his devotee's excitement. 'I am pleased with your devotion. Ask me anything you want.'

Bhasmasura said, 'My lord, grant me such a boon that if I touch anyone's head, the person is reduced to ashes in no time!' Shiva was a little confused at such a boon, but couldn't find any wickedness in Bhasmasura's expression. Moreover, Shiva is known as Bholenath because he trusts his devotees easily. So he raised his hand and blessed him with what he had wished for.

Bhasmasura felt a strange power in his hands, and he knew, he was invincible. He looked joyous at having received such a boon. He couldn't wait to test it, so he started looking around. He looked at Shiva once more and checked, 'So, if I touch anyone, he would be reduced to ashes?' Shiva nodded. 'Yes, my dear Bhasmasura. That's what you asked for!'

Then Bhasmasura let out a demonic laugh and said, 'Then, my lord, allow me to touch your head first to see whether you have given me the right boon or not!' With that, he rushed towards Shiva.

Shiva now realized Bhasmasura's true intension. He staggered back and ran for his life. He ran and ran, and Bhasmasura kept chasing him, his arms outstretched to catch him. Running for his life, Shiva reached a dense forest and hid behind some trees. Then he prayed to Vishnu for help. Vishnu heard him and rushed to help Shiva. Without wasting a moment, Vishnu took the form of a beautiful young maiden, and made his way to the earth to distract Bhasmasura.

Bhasamasura also reached the forest, but he had lost Shiva's trail. He looked everywhere carefully, scanned every inch, but couldn't get even a glimpse of the lord.

Soon enough, he found his vision glued to someone. It was a beautiful woman, plucking flowers. She was as bright as the divine apsaras and just as glorious.

Bhasmasura forgot all about Shiva and went over to the beautiful woman. He knew he wanted to marry her, not realizing that the woman was none other than Vishnu himself! Bhasmasura felt a delightful pang in his heart. He reached closer to the woman and said, 'Lady, who are you?'

'Before you ask my name, you should introduce yourself,' said the woman. Bhasmasura smiled foolishly and said, 'Oh! My name is Bhasmasura. I am an asura, and my strength is mightier than anyone! I am as strong as a god!'

'My name is Mohini,' said the woman. 'I am a dancer, and there is no one who can dance like me. I live on the outskirts of this forest with my father. I often come here to pluck flowers for my father's daily prayer.' Bhasmasura was in love with this woman at first sight. On an impulse, he blurted out, 'O Mohini, I wish to marry you. I fell in love with you the moment my eyes first rested on you. I will give you all the happiness you have ever dreamt of. Will you marry me?'

Mohini shook her head. 'I can't do that, Bhasmasura. I had promised my father that I shall marry the one who could dance like me. If you can dance like me, then I certainly can marry you. Otherwise, it is not possible.'

Bhasmasura was now in trouble. He had not danced before, but he also didn't want to lose Mohini. So he said, 'I know nothing about dancing, Mohini. But if you teach me, I can become a good dancer. Then you can marry me!'

Mohini looked at him with a smile, and finally, agreed. 'Yes, it is easy. Just follow and copy my steps and do whatever I am doing.' She set her flower basket aside and started dancing, showing

Bhasmasura what to do. He, in turn, kept copying her steps. Gradually, he started getting better and gained more confidence in himself as a dancer.

Mohini saw that Bhasmasura was too busy copying the steps, all his attention on the dancing. It was just the precise moment she had been waiting for! She leapt in the air and landed on the ground, putting her hand on her head.

Bhasmasura thought it might be a dancing step, so he also leapt in the air and landed with his hand on his head. And then it happened! A strange flinching sensation ran across Bhasmasura's veins, as if his body was burning in fire. He remembered his boon. He realized that Mohini had tricked him! But before he could scream, his body collapsed on the ground, reduced to ashes. Right then, Shiva came out of his hiding place and headed towards Mohini, who had now come to her real form of lord Vishnu.

Both the gods laughed and felt relieved – a great trouble had just been burnt to ashes!

16

THE SKIN-CHANGER

Rambha was a mighty asura, who could change himself into any animal he desired. Once, changing himself into a male buffalo, he was grazing around the forest, when his eyes fell on a female buffalo bathing in a river. It was princess Shyamala, cursed to be a buffalo. He fell in love with her and started living with her. A few months later, Shyamala gave birth to a mighty asura, and they named him Mahishasura *(mahisha means buffalo)*. He possessed such strength that could even subdue the greatest warriors on earth. He was a master of stealth and also had a mystic power - he could change himself into a giant buffalo at will. From his early days, Mahishasura was a staunch worshipper of lord Brahma. He had only one desire – to rule over heaven. But being an asura, he knew he could never accomplish such a dream without having a divine boon!

So he performed an extremely terrifying penance to please lord Brahma. Without eating or drinking for years, he kept chanting Brahma's name. And after a long wait, Brahma was appeased. He appeared before Mahishasura and asked what he desired. Mahisasura said, 'My lord, bless me with immortality!' But Brahma shook his head and said, 'I can't give you that, son. Whoever is born, must die. It is the universal law. So ask for something else.'

Mahishasura had thought Brahma would certainly grant him immortality. So he was disappointed, but quickly gathered his wit. He was puzzled about what to ask! He thought his fear was only of the gods. Except for gods, he knew he was powerful enough to defeat anyone. Men or other asuras did not stand a chance! So he said, 'My lord, bless me that I cannot be killed by any gods, asuras or men.' Brahma nodded. 'If that is what you want, then you will have it!'

Brahma granted him the boon he had asked for, and as he departed homewards, Mahishasura chuckled along. He knew that even without immortality, he was invincible. Very soon, Mahishasura became the king of the asuras, defeating everyone. Then he formed a massive army of asuras, only to rule over the world. One by one, he captured all the land across the world and became the undisputed king of the earth. And then his eyes fell on the heaven. To have heaven under his rule, he marched forward with his army of asuras to Indra's court. In a trice, he charged and defeated Indra with ease.

Indra got terrified of Mahishasura's wrath and leaving the throne empty, he ran away. Unable to find a way to defeat the mighty Mahishasura, Indra reached the Trinity (Brahma, Vishnu and Shiva) and described the terrifying experience. Brahma said, 'I never thought he would be so notorious. No god, asura or man can kill him as per the boon I gave him!'

'Hmm. What about a woman?' suggested Shiva. 'Do you think a woman can slay Mahishasura?' asked Brahma.

Vishnu nodded. 'Yes, it is possible, if the woman is none other than goddess Shakti herself.' The devas agreed on this idea. Then everyone channelized their power in one direction, and from that point emerged a ten-armed goddess, named Durga. Her beauty was unrivalled, but her anger was enough to melt down the entire universe! As soon as Durga emerged and heard of the demonic activities caused by Mahishasura, she vowed to kill him. The gods offered Durga several weapons to prepare her for the battle with the mighty asura.

Lord Vishnu gave her the Sudarshan chakra; Indra gave her his Vajra; Brahma gave her the lotus of knowledge and a bowl of amrit; Varuna gave her a conch shell; Vishwakarma gave her a mighty axe; Kubera gave her a divine cudgel; Surya and Pavan dev gave her a bow and arrow; Airavat, Indra's mount, gave her a bell; Agni gave her a sword and shield; and lastly, Shiva gave her his own trident and snake. When Durga was adorned with these weapons, the king of mountains, Himalaya, gave her a lion to ride on.

As soon as Durga was armed, she charged against Mahishasura and challenged him for a fight. But Mahishasura laughed. He wondered, when the gods and men couldn't do anything against him, what could a woman do! But he accepted the challenge. Their battle continued for nine days. Mahishasura fought very hard, threw several weapons at her, and transforming into a huge buffalo, he charged at Durga multiple times. But he was no match to her. She deflected every strike and remained unharmed.

Then, on the tenth day, when Mahishasura was tired after such a long battle, Durga got the chance she needed. She pulled out her trident and pierced Mahisasura's chest, bringing his death. Every god bowed to Durga and worshipped her as the Universal Mother. And people on earth gave her the name - Mahishasurmardini (the slayer of Mahishasura).

This is also one of the many stories behind the festival of Navaratri, where the goddess is worshipped for nine days.

17

THE MALEVOLENT BROTHERS

Shumbha and Nishumbha were two brothers - they were always together, and even created chaos on earth together. They were so malevolent that they used to torture everyone to no end. Seeking greater power, they made austerities to please Brahma. They prayed and meditated on his name for years and years, and finally managed to please him. The lord appeared in front of them and offered to grant them a boon.

They literally pleaded, 'O father of Creation, we want only one boon. We don't want to die at the hands of any man or god. Give us the strength that no man or god can become the cause of our death.'

Brahma did not see any problem in that, and thinking them to be good devotees, granted them the desired boon. Following the power that came with the boon, they marched from kingdom to kingdom, capturing thrones and kicking the kings out of their cities.

Not stopping at that, they wreaked havoc around the three worlds - heaven, earth and hell. In their drunkenness of power, they defeated everyone who tried to oppose them. No god could stand against their might and the brothers remained unconquerable. They raised a huge army of asuras and appointed Chanda and Munda – two sinister-looking asuras – to lead the army. Together, they started tormenting their subjects, as clamour and chaos reigned everywhere.

One day, while on their usual conquest of new lands, Chanda and Munda saw goddess Parvati from a distance. They were totally enchanted with her mesmerizing beauty. They knew what they had to do!

They returned to their kingdom and sang praises of goddess Parvati's beauty to Shumbha and Nishumbha. Such was the charm of just the description, that both the brothers couldn't even imagine what she would be like in real. And they immediately desired to marry her. So, they sent Chanda and Munda with a marriage proposal. Delighted, the two army generals walked over to the goddess and conveyed the proposal of Shumbha and Nishumbha. Parvati was so enraged that she drove them out of her palace.

This rejection made Shumbha and Nishumbha furious. They sent their entire army of asuras to abduct the goddess. But Parvati wasn't any ordinary goddess. She was the true form of goddess Shakti. As soon as she saw the asura-army marching forth, with Chanda and Munda leading them, she incarnated as goddess Chandi. Such was her wrath that she wiped out everyone single-handedly, and killed Chanda and Munda. For that, she came to be known as Chamunda. When the news reached Shumbha and Nishumbha, they were so furious that they decided to fight the goddess.

Soon enough, they reached and challenged Parvati for a fight. The goddess was ready for that as well. She knew this would happen and was prepared in advance. She incarnated as goddess Kaushiki, and started fighting with them in the battlefield. The battle went on for days, and Shumbha and Nishumbha couldn't do any harm to Kaushiki. She, on her part, fought valiantly. The brothers had believed that they would be invincible because of the boon given to them by Brahma. But they had forgotten that they had wished not to get killed by men or gods. They had not wished protection from any goddess! Nishumbha got slain by Kaushiki first. As soon as he died, a powerful demon emerged out of his corpse. But Kaushiki managed to wipe out the demon.

Seeing his dear brother fall dead in front of his own eyes, Shumbha started fighting more violently. But each of his attempt went in vain. He couldn't inflict any harm to Kaushiki. Instead, the goddess deflected every strike, countered every move. At last, she split his head into two. The very moment she destroyed Shumbha and Nishumbha, the three worlds were free from evil. Goddess Kaushiki had restored peace in all the three worlds.

18
INVINCIBILITY IN BLOOD

Like Chanda and Munda, Raktabeej was also a gruesome militant in the army of Shumbha and Nishumbha. His sole aim seemed to be making lives of gods difficult.

He wanted to be the most powerful in the world, and that wish made him frantic. He could do anything to achieve that goal and the only way was to perform penance and get a protective boon for himself. So that is what he did. He prayed to Brahma for years after years.

Like every other time, when Brahma saw the sincerity with which Raktabeej was meditating on him, he appeared and offered him a boon of his choice.

Raktabeej was delighted at the offer, but was not sure what he should ask for. He said, 'Bless me with a boon that if my blood ever spills onto the ground, a thousand times more powerful Raktabeej would generate from each drop of my blood.'

'Whatever you wish, my dear devotee,' blessed Brahma and went back to his abode.

Not much later, Raktabeej dashed towards heaven and challenged Indra for battle. After all, who needed an army! Every drop of his blood that would spill, would give birth to a new and more powerful Raktabeej.

On the other hand, the devas accepted the challenge and started battling with him. They were not aware of his boon, and whenever they thought they had killed the asura, thousands of more powerful Raktabeejs would appear from his dripping blood.

The devas knew they couldn't stand against the asura with this powerful boon. Indra, being defeated in such a way, had to flee from heaven. The devas gathered and prayed to goddess Durga for protection.

The problem at hand was indeed a tricky one, and they had to find a smart way out of it. The goddess took on the incarnation of goddess Kali and waged battle against Raktabeej.

As soon as Raktabeej saw Kali, he turned all his anger towards her. He thought, 'Will this woman be able to harm me? No!'

Kali fought hard, but every time she would kill him, thousands of Raktabeejs would appear again. The number grew so immensely that Kali had to fight for a long time; and still, she couldn't find a way to end Raktabeej's life.

When Kali got tired and angry with millions of Raktabeejs around her, she understood that this asura could not be killed in a straight off battle. So, she came up with an idea.

She produced a big bowl, and each time she would slash one Raktabeej, she would collect its blood in the bowl and drink it.

She kept doing this for as long as it took, to ensure no blood spilled and touched the ground. Once that was done, no more Raktabeejs could emerge out again.

Finally, Kali killed the last Raktabeej. Drinking its blood, she wiped out the mean asura and his evil activities from the earth, restoring peace everywhere.

19

BORN OUT OF ASHES

Long ago, lord Shiva had gotten enraged over Kamadeva (the god of love), as he had dared to break Shiva's meditation. Shiva thus opened his third eye, and an insurmountable flame flared out of it. As a result of which, Kamadeva was burnt to ashes. Instantly, out of those ashes, a giant asura emerged, who had the strength of the gods! His name was Bhandasura. As soon as Bhandasura came to life, he set his eyes on Shiva. Seeing his charismatic form, he became a staunch devotee of lord Shiva. With time, he started worshipping Shiva with all his heart.

A few years later, like it happens with all the asuras, his heart also got desirous of become mightier than everyone. He wanted to be all powerful, and equipped with his bhakti for Shiva, he knew he could do it! He also knew that the gods would never bless him with immortality, so he wove a great plan. He started meditating to please Shiva, holding a desire that the lord would grant him a boon. Shiva was pleased with Bhandasura's sincere devotion, and appearing before him, he said, 'Bhandasura, I am pleased with your love and dedication towards me. I have come here to bless you! Tell me, what do you want?' Bhandasura had been waiting for this grand moment. He bowed down to Shiva and said, 'My lord, if you are really pleased with my devotion, then bless me that no man, asura or god would ever dare to fight against me. And if they do, they would forfeit half of their strength and masculinity to me.' Shiva granted him his desired boon. Ready with a plan already, Bhandasura immediately formed a great army of terrible asuras and charged at heaven. All asuras lived with the motive of winning over heaven, it seemed. This time, they challenged Indra for a battle.

Indra, however, wasn't aware of Bhandasura's mighty boon. Just as he came out to fight against Bhandasura, he lost half of his strength to Bhandasura's own power. Precious half of his strength now lost, Indra felt weak before Bhandasura. In the end, it was an easy win for that wretched asura. He shooed the devas out of heaven and claiming himself as the new king, he ascended the throne. There he remained for six thousand years and tortured the devas, humans and everyone in general. He was so mean to everyone, that the three worlds were tired of his atrocities. Getting offended by Bhandasura's evil attempts and to regain his throne back, Indra, along with the entourage of devas, reached Shiva and described their miserable situation. But they found no help from Shiva. The lord did warn them that no man or god could stand against Bhandasura, thanks to his boon. 'You all should seek the help of goddess Shakti,' said Shiva. 'Only she can help you out of this troublesome situation.' As advised, all the devas prayed to Shakti, hoping that she would help them out.

When goddess Shakti appeared and heard how Bhandasura had spread his tyranny across the worlds, she was infuriated. She said, 'You need not worry about a mere asura like him. I will end his evil plans and restore peace. You devas will get back your heaven soon.' Then she incarnated as Devi Lalita and formed a huge army of goddesses for wiping out Bhandasura and his army of asuras. When the asura saw Devi Lalita entering his kingdom, Bhandasura laughed. He roared, 'When the gods couldn't stand against my strength, they decided to send a goddess to kill me! How funny!'

'A goddess is enough to wipe you out!' roared Devi Lalita, challenging him for a fight. Bhandasura mocked her as he came to the battleground, wielding multiple weapons in his hands. But Bhandasura had conveniently forgotten that his boon would help if he was battling a man or god – not women or goddesses. And without his boon, he really was a mere asura in front of Devi Lalita.

No matter how much Bhandasura tried to defeat the goddess, he just couldn't. And chopping the evil asura's head off, Devi Lalita finished the task she had set out for. After Bhandasura's death, the gods started living peacefully in their abode and claimed Devi Lalita as the peace-bringer to the gods. Devi Lalita is worshipped across the entire country with another name - Tripura Sundari.

20

THE FEVER DEMON

Once, lord Shiva was lost in his divine meditation for a long time. He got so soaked in it that a tremendous amount of heat generated out of his body.

The heat was so radiant, so impactful that Shiva perspired tremendously. His body trembled, as he was fully drenched in sweat.

It was at that very moment - when a drop of his sweat dropped on the ground - that a terrible looking wicked asura was born out of it. He was born with a sly grin on his lips.

He was Jvarasura – a demon who had such magnificent strength that he could make anyone fall ill. He was infamous for spreading diseases, fever and cold.

No sooner did he find Shiva next to him than he rushed towards the lord and spread fever into his body. Now, Shiva felt a strange shiver run down his spine. As his body temperature rose high, even before he could show his wrath to Jvarasura, he fell to the ground like a sick mortal.

Jvarasura laughed a mad laugh, proud of his ability to handicap the most powerful of gods. He left Shiva in his terrible state, and dashed towards heaven.

Reaching the abode of Indra, he spread his fever across the entire heaven. And before the devas could think of fighting the asura out, they all fell sick. They lost all their strength to stand against the asura. The fever made them so weak and frail that they couldn't even stand on their own feet. They writhed like ailing people.

Every mighty god was soon defeated by this nasty asura spreading fever and sickness. What could they do! They started praying to Brahma for help, who was also enfeebled by Jvarasura's fever.

Wriggling into his great lotus, Brahma could say nothing, only muttered something like, 'Pray to goddess Katyayani.'

Folding their hands, all the gods then prayed to Devi Katyayani, who was another form of goddess Shakti.

When Devi Katyayani appeared before them and was told about Javasura's despicable activities, she swore to take revenge.

Right then, she incarnated as Devi Shitala - literally meaning the cool one - and marched towards the asura's residence.

As soon as Jvarasura found a goddess next to his dwelling place, he charged and spread fever towards her. But Devi Shitala knew how to subdue the fever. She was the goddess of coolness, and with her might, she spread her bone-chilling cold across Jvarasura's body, freezing him into an ice-cube.

When Jvarasura couldn't hold the sheer chill of Shitala's coolness, he begged for mercy.

Devi Shitala felt pity for Jvarasura, and ordered him to become her slave forever.

Then the goddess cured the fever of the Trinity and other devas, and from then on, Jvarasura became the slave of Devi Shitala. Since then, whenever people fall sick on earth, they pray to Devi Shitala to break their rising temperature.

21

THE ARTISAN

The story of Mayasura is found in the great epic - *the Mahabharata.*

Kauravas (the one hundred sons of Dhritarashtra) drove the Pandavas (the five sons of Pandu) out of Hastinapur using the conspiracy of their uncle Shakuni. That is when Krishna – the best friend and counsellor of Pandavas – suggested to make Khandavaprastha their new home.

Pandavas always trusted Krishna the most. So without further delay, Yudhishtir, Bheem, Arjun, Nakul and Sahadev decided to go with Krishna's suggestion.

During that time, Khandavaprastha was a dense forest, which was mainly a deserted, forsaken land acquired by the Nagas – the snake-people. Their leader, Takshak had befriended a sly asura, named Mayasura, who had several mystic powers and lived in Khandavaprastha forest along with the Nagas.

Long ago, Mayasura had performed a grand penance, and pleased Brahma by his devotion. The lord had granted him an unrivalled skill in architecture as a boon. And thus Mayasura became a great artisan, who could create things almost out of nowhere, like the creator, Brahma himself.

Now, in the Khandavaprastha forest, Mayasura and Takshak Naga made the forest so miserable for animals that no one dared to graze into it. Even those who earlier lived there had to flee from Khandavaprastha.

When Pandavas, along with lord Krishna, reached Khandavaprastha forest, Krishna said to Arjun, 'My dear Arjun, this place is deserted. So, if you burn down the entire forest, you all can build your kingdom here.'

Arjun did that. He drew an arrow and using his bow named Gandiv, shot fire-arrows around the forest. The forest soon burned down to ashes.

Now, the wicked Nagas, who had made the place miserable for other animals, started burning down in that scorching fire. Even their leader Takshak had to scamper away from there to find a safe place.

But Mayasura couldn't flee, and remained alone in the forest with a raging fire around him. To save his life, he got out of the forest and stood angrily before Krishna and Arjun. Arjun, the greatest archer of all times, pulled out his bow Gandiv and aimed an arrow at him. He wanted to kill the asura and make the place good enough for building their city there.

At this, Mayasura got so frightened that he fell to Arjun's feet, begging for mercy.

Krishna, however, asked Arjun to forgive Mayasura. He then ordered the mystic asura to build a marvellous palace for the Pandavas, right on the ground of Khandavaprastha.

Mayasura didn't dare to go against the mighty Krishna, and waving his hands in the air, he produced a huge palace. It was made of crystals and glittering gems. It was so marvellous and magical that everyone was wonderstruck looking at it.

It came to be known as Maya Sabha or the Palace of Illusions.

Krishna and Pandavas were delighted to have such a unique palace for themselves. They applauded Mayasura's mystic power before letting him go free to live his life.

22

WHEN THE GODS MERGE

Guheshwara was an ardent devotee of Brahma. He always wanted to become supreme in strength. He knew, praying to Brahma could earn him a boon. He could use the god's blessings to become invincible! But he was well aware of the fact that Brahma would never bless immortality to anyone. He had told far too many that this was not a boon he could grant. So they knew they should be prepared with a plan B. Thinking very hard, he plotted a good plan and started performing a tough penance to please the lord. The strength of his austerity made such an impact on Brahma that he couldn't stop himself from coming over to him. As soon as Brahma appeared, he asked Guheshwara, 'My dear devotee, I am pleased with you. I have come here to grant you a boon. Ask me anything your heart craves for!'

Guheshwara slyly said, 'My Lord, you are not going to give anyone the boon of immortality anyway!' 'Yes, my child. I cannot. If you are seeking the same, I can't help you. You must ask something that is not against the law of nature.' 'Then grant me such a boon that no god or goddess of heaven could ever become my death, not even the mortals of the earth.' Brahma never disheartened his devotees. So, he granted Guheshwara the boon he had desired for. Getting this mighty boon, Guheshwara's asura instincts were kindled. He started defeating all the kings around the world. He even tormented scholars and learned men to no end. He slaughtered everyone who tried to oppose him. In the end, there remained no peace anywhere – only chaos. Most of the people scampered away from their homes. They were scared for their lives and families. The rest of them kept praying to the gods for help.

Now, in heaven, the gods heard people's cries and pleaded to Brahma to do something about this. They noticed that Guheshwara was being so evil, because he feared nobody. He had Brahma's boon and the fearlessness was the root of his evil. But Brahma shook his head and said, 'I gave him a boon and now he is abusing it. But the boon is so powerful that no god can wipe him out. Even I am incompetent before him. I can do nothing in this matter. You may seek the help of Shiva and Vishnu. Hope they can do something about it.' All the gods then scurried to Shiva and Vishnu, describing the miserable situation of the people on earth. 'But Brahma blessed him that no god from heaven could kill him!' Shiva said to Vishnu. 'We can never slay that wretched asura!' Vishnu nodded, but he also came up with an ingenious plan! He said, 'What if we merge our bodies into one! Then we are not one god, but two! And then, with your valiant strength and my sheer wit, we could knock the asura down!'

'What a great idea!' Shiva agreed. The other gods also saw a ray of hope in it. Then the right side of Shiva – with the crescent moon, river Ganga, the trident, the damru and half of his third eye – joined with Vishnu's left side that possessed the Sudarshana chakra, the mace and his crown with the peacock feather. This new god was called Harihara [a form with both, Vishnu (Hari) and Shiva (Hara)]. As they had planned, with his sheer power, Harihara galloped over to Guheshwara, challenging him for a battle. Guheshwara laughed and said, 'Don't you know, I am invincible! I cannot be killed by any god!' Harihara smiled dramatically and said, 'Let's see, how much your boon can protect you from us. We are not one god, but two!'

But Guheshwara didn't care much about Harihara's words, as he was totally convinced he could never be defeated. And then, drawing his sword, he charged at Harihara. But Harihara was no ordinary being! As Guheshwara closed in, wielding his sword, Harihara kicked him so hard that the asura skidded a mile off and toppled. He rose and charged again, but no matter how hard he tried to defeat the god, he couldn't stand against Harihara's strength. At last, when Guheshwara's strength slackened and he was tired, Harihara wielded his trident and was about to pierce it right through the asura's chest, when the asura fell to the god's feet, begging for mercy. He had realized he couldn't beat this new god. He said, 'Don't kill me, O mighty lord. I apologize for my misdeeds. I am guilty, but don't kill me. Please show some mercy and take me under your wing.'

Harihara felt pity. He placed his feet over Guheshwara's head, pushing him down to the ground. Guheshwara was sent to the lower realm of the world - the Paataal Lok and relieved the earth from his demonic presence.